COURAGE in the Knight

Story of the Month
Newsletter Series

by

STACIA RAE LOWE

Illustrations by Magdalena Baughman

Thank you!

Adam, for sparking my love of writing with our snail-mail letters back and forth to each other in the early years. It was during that time, with those letters, that the idea of writing a book together was born. Publishing that book, *Hidden Hope*, was when I first realized my love of writing books. And now we get to discover God's purpose and future for our writing together, which is one of my favorite things to do with you!

Mom, you have been my constant support through this writing journey. (We both know that between you and Dad, you're the one who gave me my grammar-loving genes!) You have put in countless hours editing all my books, and providing constant encouragement. I'm better at this book-writing thing because of you.

Angie, my writing partner, my lifelong friend. I love bouncing ideas off each other. You are the one who gave me the idea for this *Story of the Month* series, which seems like such a long time ago! Your big-picture dreams balance out my detail-oriented, slow-and-steady progress, to create well-balanced writing for both of us.

Table of CONTENTS

Newsletter Installments
April ~ October 2025

1

THE SOUNDS ALL around him went from muted and muffled to extreme and deafening in a matter of minutes. The only change that Ethan noticed was the arrival of Uncle Alan's family, but those eight members of the family were loud enough to scare away a bear.

"We're here!"

Ethan heard his uncle's booming baritone voice from the

back of the house, and still felt the need to escape. *I'm pretty sure the whole neighborhood knows you're here, Uncle Alan.* Ethan kept his thoughts to himself, but that didn't stop him from sneaking into the room above the garage to be by himself.

Thanksgiving was always an ordeal in the Lewis household, and this year was no different. It usually started with Ethan's dad's family. Uncle Alan, Aunt Judy and the six cousins brought chaos with them wherever they went.

Grandma Anne usually kept to herself throughout the day, but sometimes her hearing aids didn't work, if she remembered to wear them at all. Occasionally, she would talk to herself so loudly that she'd end up by herself when everyone else vacated the area, not able to hear their own conversations. Last year she hollered during Dad's Thanksgiving meal prayer, "What is he saying? I don't have my ears on!" But she's pretty harmless the rest of the time.

It's when Ethan's aunts show up every year that the party can really get out of hand. His mom's twin sisters, Jenny and Penny, had a reputation of being cranky, middle-aged spinsters. One year they walked through the front door arguing about who knows what. The bickering lasted through dinner all the way until they left the house after dessert was cleared away from the table. They hadn't even thought about offering to help their sister clean up the kitchen, but the rest of the family was fine pitching in a little more just so those grouchy women would leave!

Ethan was used to his family drama, but that didn't mean he liked it. He preferred quiet time by himself, just him and his guitar, rather than being another number in the crowd . . . even if that crowd was his own family.

Music pulsed through his veins. Ethan was never more than a reach away from his guitar.

This year Aunt Penny brought her new boyfriend and his three kids, which made Aunt Jenny jealous. She wouldn't admit it, but everyone could tell. It was bad enough when it was just the twins squawking, but now there were four more who didn't know when to put a cork in it!

When it was time to eat, Ethan's little brother Wyatt knew exactly where to find him. Ethan could hear him tromping up the stairs before barging into the guest room where he was hiding.

"Mom said it's time for dinner."

"Okay, I'm coming." Ethan responded quickly with his words, but his body was not so fast to follow.

"She said now." Wyatt was always running everywhere he went, kicking furniture, bouncing off the walls. He was the complete opposite of his brother. Ethan preferred to approach his day with much contemplation and consideration.

There wasn't a rushed bone in his body.

As soon as he made it to the dining room, his Uncle Alan said, "There he is. Now let's eat!"

"Thank you for joining us, son." Ethan's mom turned to her husband and asked, "Hon, will you please say grace?"

"Let's bow our heads." As Ethan's dad extended his hand to Grammy and his wife, a ripple effect of linked hands zippered down the table as the whole family joined together in prayer. "Heavenly Father, thank you for this day we can all turn our hearts to gratitude. Please bless the hands that have prepared this delicious-looking meal, and bless it to the nourishment of our bodies. Amen."

Over the next hour, the Thanksgiving turkey was inhaled, the yams topped with crispy-brown marshmallows were consumed, and there wasn't a single black olive remaining. In the same way the food disappeared, so did the family's manners.

Ethan sat next to his cousin Jeffrey, the only two boys who didn't have to sit at the kids' table, since they were the oldest of the cousins. Ethan's twelve years seemed more mature than some of the adults sitting around the table.

Finishing the last bite of his banana bread, he turned to his mom and asked, "May I please be excused?"

"Yes, sweetheart. That's fine. We'll have pie a little later."

Calmly but quickly Ethan stood, pushed his chair in, and fled to the living room where he had left his guitar, recalling his anxiety when everyone began to show up at his house that morning. When they had arrived, he immediately retreated to the safety of the garage guest room, forgetting to take his guitar with him.

Unfortunately, that meant that now he wasn't able to move fast enough, after grabbing his instrument, to escape before anyone else joined him in the living room. His limp slowed him down too much.

He was used to maneuvering with a crooked gate ever since he had gotten his leg braces removed several years prior. The obnoxious reminder of his complicated childhood still had an effect on Ethan.

Daily discouragement and embarrassment were just the tip of the iceberg. It was when those feelings turned into a crippling anxiety that Ethan's physical limitations paled in comparison.

2

WHEN ETHAN WAS two years old, his parents received the most devastating news they were never expecting.

"Your son has cancer."

Ethan had been diagnosed with acute lymphoblastic leukemia. This fatal blood disease ravaged his little body in a matter of months, so much so that by the time of his diagnosis the doctors had said his heart was at risk of failing.

That phone call was the beginning of a three-year journey that turned Ethan's world upside down. From blood transfusions to steroids and chemotherapy, Ethan's cancer treatments were extensive and painful. In some cases anesthesia was administered so the poisonous chemo could be injected directly into his spinal fluid. A procedure no parent would ever want their child to experience.

Most days their baby wasn't even able to express the kind of torment he was feeling. How could he put words to the pain when he only had a limited vocabulary at that age? By the end of the years of treatment, Ethan had endured the pain for the majority of his young life.

It was the only thing he really knew.

One of the side effects of the chemo was bone loss in his legs. It wasn't until his parents noticed how often he was tripping over his own feet that they asked his oncologist if it was something to be worried about.

"I'm giving you a referral to go see a specialist. He will likely have Ethan wear leg braces to help support his weakening joints." It was just one more complication to add to the list of already overwhelming details of their son's cancer.

But they wouldn't stop.

Every injection, every nausea pill, every sleepless night was one step closer to their child's recovery and ultimate goal of healing. This was their daily prayer. This was their community's daily prayer . . . that one day Ethan would be cancer free.

Thanksgiving was only one day of the year; however, Ethan's family lived every day with a mindset of gratefulness knowing that modern medicine had cured his diseased body before the disease took his life.

That infamous phone call turning his reality into a nightmare was over ten years ago, now. But there were still those days when Ethan wished he didn't have a crippled leg as a permanent reminder of the walking miracle that he was.

His parents liked to refer to Ethan's treatment scars as proof of his victory over cancer. Ethan, however, would rather just forget the whole ordeal.

"Are you going to play something for us?" Aunt Jenny was apparently right on his heels out of the dining room, the first of the crowd following him to fight over couch space and arm chair pillows.

"I'm the man of the house . . . well, his brother at least," Uncle Alan bellowed, "that recliner is mine."

"Yes dear," Aunt Judy replied, "we all know your claim to that chair every year."

"Ethan, play something for us." He couldn't even tell who suggested it this time as three of his cousins zipped across the floor, nearly crashing into him.

"What are you waiting for? Is it too early to request Christmas songs?" Laughter erupted after Aunt Jenny's comment.

Despite the enjoyment and light-hearted teasing going on around him, Ethan began to feel dizzy. Was the room swaying? The only thing he could do to stop his world from spinning out of control was to play.

His instrument was like a suit of armor protecting him from the threats surrounding him.

Without another thought, Ethan closed his eyes. Feeling piercing stares like lasers burning into his skin, all the voices blending into one constant echo rattling around in his brain, he knew what he had to do.

Ethan lifted up his guitar with his left hand, holding it by the neck of the instrument. With his eyes still closed, he slid his finger down a single smooth string as if it were a slicing blade that would protect against attackers. Gliding the fabric strap through his palm, and guiding it over his head onto one shoulder, Ethan secured his guitar, his shield firmly in place.

He imagined the body of his instrument guarding him as if it were the breastplate of a royal knight's armor. Ethan removed his guitar pick from in between the strings, holding it in place as the king's soldier would carry his sword prepared to advance.

He was ready for battle. No weapon could harm him now. No threat of anxiety could penetrate the barrier between him and the energy pulsating off the expectant crowd.

Family pressures to perform faded into vapors as Ethan began to play. A single strum of the first chord transported him to another time in history.

3

"HARK, ALL YE assembled! Let silence reign in this our Royal Presence, as we bestow upon a worthy subject the highest honor of our realm!"

In the presence of royalty, honored by the king, Ethan couldn't believe it. And yet, his own confidence and pride was as true as the jeweled sword in the hand of the king standing before him.

"Rise, Ethan Lewis of Edinburgh, true and loyal subject!" The tenor voice of King Charles II of England carried Ethan away from his thoughts and back into this momentous moment. He stood, noticing the searing pain radiating through his leg. His most recent battle wound. As he approached the throne where the king stood, Ethan's limp slowed each step. But the cost of protecting his king and country was worth it. Such a minor setback wouldn't hold him back.

"By the grace of Almighty God, and by the divine right vested in Our Royal Person, We, King Charles II of England, Sovereign of England, Scotland and Ireland, and Defender of the Faith, do stand here this day to elevate one whose deeds have proven him deserving."

In this moment, Ethan couldn't remember a time when fear ever controlled his decisions. His loyalty to the king in service of his country was a response to his faith in God, which had always been at the forefront of his mind.

"For your valor displayed in battle, for your unwavering loyalty to the Crown, and for your steadfast courage in the face of adversity, both in times of war and peace, you shall receive this day this noble honor. Therefore, Ethan Lewis of Edinburgh, kneel and receive that which your merit has earned."

Hundreds of guests were in attendance for this royal ceremony honoring his accomplishments.

Even the rich tapestries hanging on the walls of this grand hall spoke of the celebration Ethan felt as he reverently lowered himself to the knighting stool.

"In the name of the Father, and of the Son, and of the Holy Spirit, I dub thee Knight!" Ethan blinked away the sheen of joyful tears beginning to cloud his vision. "Go forth, Sir Ethan Lewis, and let your deeds continue to reflect the greatness of this realm. May God grant you strength and wisdom in all your endeavors."

The sound of applause and cheers welcomed the royal trumpet fanfare concluding the ceremony. As Ethan stood to his feet, he closed his eyes to soak it all in. He couldn't stop the smile that reached far beyond his eyes, into his soul.

Ethan opened his eyes as the applause was beginning to die down, only to find his guitar strapped to his chest, ringing with the final chord of the song he had just performed for his family.

Wait, did I just play an entire song for everyone? Ethan was still trying to put the pieces together when his aunt burst out with a squeal.

"Oh, Ethan, that was beautiful!" Aunt Jenny exclaimed while rushing over to Ethan to give him a bear hug. "I never knew you could play the guitar so well!"

"Thank you?" Ethan responded with more of a question in his tone. He had zero recollection of the song he had just played for the group, but apparently his audience had no clue.

The chaos of the family holiday celebration had returned to its anticipated decibel, everyone going back to their own agendas for the day.

What had just happened? The last thing Ethan could remember was the crowd cheering and trumpets sounding. Did his own music seriously just transport him back and forth from another life? He could have sworn he'd just time warped from centuries before. Even though he wasn't confident whether or not that was real or if it was all just a dream, he was sure of one thing.

Serving as a knight for the royal kingdom was much better than this life, where anxiety seemed to consume his every thought . . . and it was his music that took him there.

OVER THE NEXT two weeks Ethan couldn't get the knighting ceremony out of his head. Some days he rode the high of that memory like a cloud, carried above the everyday worries that plagued him so often. Not even his limp could make him trip and fall back down to earth.

Christmas decorations began to light Main Street in the evenings, and carols rang over the radio, reminding Ethan of the fanfare from his celebration with the trumpets and bells ringing out in jubilee. It wasn't until one Saturday afternoon when he was shopping with his mom to find the perfect gifts for his dad and little brother that the noise of the crowd got to him.

"I was just talking with Mrs. Hanson about your Christmas concert next week." Ethan's mom continued the one-sided conversation before realizing that her son wasn't listening. "Sweetheart, did you hear me?"

"Oh yeah, sorry . . . the Christmas concert." And then it registered. "Wait! Concert? What concert?"

"Son . . ." she said patiently, waiting for his full attention. "You know, you're performing your guitar solo for the winter concert at school. Mrs. Hanson was just telling me how beautiful it sounded when she heard you playing after school on Thursday. She said the two of you spoke about the concert."

"Right." Ethan tried replaying the conversation in his mind. He remembered Mrs. Hanson approaching him when he was playing his guitar, but he could not remember anything after that. *I don't even remember what I was playing.*

She pressed a little further, hoping to spark his memory. "Hark! The Herald Angels Sing."

HARK!

It was all coming back to him. That single word, and he was back in the royal hall, bowed before King Charles II. The jeweled sword. The knighting stool. He must have started playing the Christmas carol at the memory of the king's announcement, not realizing Mrs. Hanson was listening to him!

"You do remember speaking with Mrs. Hanson about playing in the Christmas concert, right?"

"Yeah."

No!

Ethan had no recollection of the conversation, but apparently, he had committed to playing in front of the entire school! Immediately, his palms began sweating. His heart was racing, and he began to sway, grabbing onto his mom's arm so he wouldn't trip over his bad leg. This was not the time to make a complete fool of himself in the middle of a crowded mall of holiday shoppers.

"Son! Are you okay? Let's find you a seat." She guided him over to a tall circle table and chairs right outside the Cinnabon counter in the food court.

"I'm okay, Mom. Sorry. My leg is just acting up again." He didn't want to tell her the real reason he was feeling dizzy, like he was about to pass out.

"Hon, I know you sometimes get nervous to play in front of people."

Sometimes? Ethan thought to himself.

"But I watched you play for the family on Thanksgiving. Your music was soaring, and it was lifting everyone else up right there with you! Your eyes were closed, but I could see the joy in your smile as you played." Moms always know their children best. "Maybe you just need to play with your eyes closed. If you can't see the audience, they might not have that crippling effect on you."

Ethan thought about it. His mom might have a point. Could it be as easy as closing his eyes while he played his guitar to take on the bravery of a knight again?

"Besides," his mom continued, bringing Ethan back to reality, "you are so much stronger than you think. You are the bravest boy I know!"

His pulse slowed and he wasn't sweating anymore. Ethan felt calm and relaxed, back to normal. Now, he just wanted to get home as soon as possible to test out his theory.

5

BUSTING THROUGH THE front door, racing down the hall, and practically removing his bedroom door from its hinges made up for the mile-long car ride back home from the mall that seemed to last, "Forrr . . . evvv . . . ver."

"Slow down, Ethan!" his mom called out as she gracefully closed the front door behind her. In an effort to be the patient parent she reminded her son, "We walk in the house, thank you!"

Ethan's mom walked over to the coat rack where she hung her purse, simultaneously hooking her keys on the engraved key holder hanging on the wall that read, "Home Sweet Home." In a quieter voice, with an audience of just herself now, she finished her thought, "My goodness! You'd think you were on your way to go save the world with the speed you were running." The sound of her son's door slamming closed adequately punctuated her remark.

With his back up against the door, Ethan scanned his room for the briefest moment, just to see what he would be escaping if his plan worked. With a deep breath he walked over to the bottom bunk, tripping on his little brother's dirty clothes from the day before. His guitar lay where it was left with the pillows, favorite blanket, and forgotten stuffed animals. The magical instrument patiently waited to be brought to life again.

Before lifting the possible portal, Ethan reverently slid his fingers up the neck. The feel of the smooth wood on the backside gave him instant relief. Comfort and safety, and yet on the opposite side the thin strings nearly sliced his fingertips with deadly accuracy. The blade of his sword holding a delicate power to pierce the heart of any man.

He plucked a single string, the rich tone filling the air with a tangible peace. Bringing his guitar to his chest, Ethan could feel the note still pulsing through the instrument, a reminder of the magic that radiated from his shield.

Every time he wore his guitar Ethan felt protected against the threats of the world. His heart was both guarded by the wooden shield and exposed by the magic of its music, drawing others into a moment of glory and peace.

*"Hark! The herald angels sing,
glory to the newborn King."*

The words to the old carol sang out in his heart as Ethan played the song on his guitar. He closed his eyes to engage with the music. Between verse and chorus, the words penetrated his soul.

"Hail the heaven-born Prince of Peace!"

The more he played, the more Ethan felt that heavenly peace ringing true. The melody took his thoughts back to the presence of the king. How could it be that playing in front of a room full of strangers terrified him, but playing for the king didn't scare him one bit? And then it hit him.

Heavenly peace!

Could that be the difference? It was a harmony from heaven giving his music wings to play for the King!

6

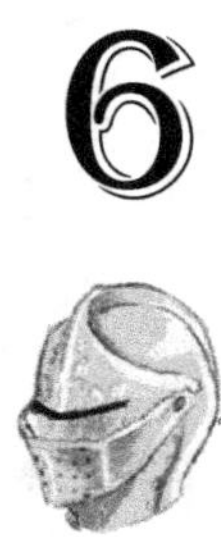

"HUZZAH!"

Immediately, Ethan opened his eyes to find the grand ballroom crowded with a flurry of Christmas decorating, the hustle and bustle of servants preparing for the annual Christmas ball.

More startling was the sight of King Charles standing and cheering with enthusiastic applause for Ethan's performance.

"A knight, *and* a musician!" The king exclaimed, "I'm not sure which I appreciate more! Oh how I love the merriment of the Christmas season! I don't recognize that carol you played, but I do enjoy it so! The music from your baroque guitar brings a festive energy to the castle. We must have more of it!"

Hoping his expression of shock didn't betray his confidence,

Ethan quickly responded, "Thank you, Your Majesty! Your praise is humbling."

Ethan continued lightly strumming his guitar, trying to think of the oldest Christmas carol he knew. The king wanted more of his music, so he transitioned into the only song that came to mind.

"Ah, yes! 'Oh Come, All Ye Faithful'. One of my favorites." The Merry Monarch was delighted with the familiar tune.

As Ethan gave the king somewhat of a personal concert, he was able to perform without a second thought of nervous anxiety. The music flowed through his fingers so naturally. He didn't even have to think about it.

Music ran through Ethan's veins. It was so much a part of who he was that he didn't even notice when he came to the end of that carol. He just began creating a new melody that partnered so well with the chords and rhythm he'd been playing for the king.

Ethan caught a glimmer of light behind where King Charles stood. When he focused on the source of the light, he saw the flickering of a single candle illuminating one corner of the ballroom. Then he saw another. And another.

Ethan gradually looked around the room as he played, noticing servants lighting hundreds of candles in decoration. Such a peaceful glow began to fill the room with warmth, as if each individual flame could warm the soul with Christmas spirit.

It reminded him of the little, white twinkle lights that his mom used each year to decorate all the doorways of every room in the house during Christmastime. Without realizing it, Ethan's guitar hummed to the tune of Silent Night.

"Silent night. Holy night.
All is calm. All is bright."

The glimmer of that first candle captured his attention again. Ethan squinted his eyes and slowly began spinning around to see all the candles in the room blend together, making a single glow of bright light. Just like the lyrics of the song.

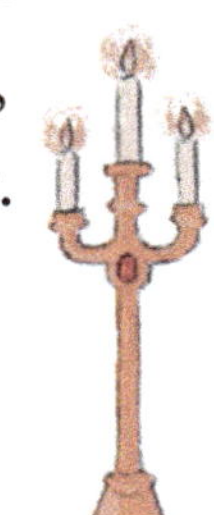

7

A KNOCK ON his bedroom door startled Ethan. Opening his eyes he turned to see his mom slowly peeking her head inside the door, the soft glow of the white twinkle lights above her head.

"Sweetheart, are you okay?"

"Yeah, Mom. I'm fine." Ethan assured her.

"After what happened at the mall . . . and then you just stormed off to your room so quickly . . . I was worried."

"I just had an idea for a song that I wanted to try. That's all."

"Okay, hon," his mom concluded hesitantly, "if you're sure."

"Thanks, Mom. I'm actually good."

The confidence in his tone convinced her of the truth. "Well, I'm glad to hear that." After a brief pause she continued. "I'm going to go start working on dinner. I'll let you know when it's ready. Dad just came in from working out in the garage, so it won't be too long."

As she backed out of the doorway, gently closing the door as she left, Ethan thought about what he had assured his mom. After his visit with the king, he truly was feeling good. Not only about playing in the recital, but in his confidence as a musician.

I performed for a KING! And he loved it!

After his interaction with royalty, without any trace of anxiety, Ethan knew he could perform anywhere.

Unfortunately, that hopeful mindset didn't follow him into the next week. Each day closer to the concert brought with it a new concern. What if he forgot a verse? He wouldn't have to play *and* sing, would he? What if his leg gave out and he collapsed in front of the entire auditorium?

It was as if that last thought had caused a spiral effect in Ethan's mobility at school that final week leading up to the concert. Not only was he nervous to mess up in front of the whole school, but now his leg wouldn't even work! He couldn't get the image of falling flat on his face out of his mind. When had he ever tripped and stumbled so many times in a day?

"This is so not fair!"

The second Ethan realized he had said the words out loud, he looked around the hallway outside his English class to see if anyone heard him. And of course, it was right as two girls were passing by.

He saw them whisper behind their hands to each other, and giggle.

"Great!" His second outburst got another reaction from the girls as they looked back at him.

Just great!

At home that afternoon Ethan decided he would channel all his nervous energy into his guitar, hoping he could spark some of its magic in the last two days before the big day.

Over and over again he played the song. Eventually, his wrist and shoulder were sore from holding the guitar for so long. The callouses on his fingertips turned into fresh blisters. And to top it all off, nothing he did activated his guitar's magical portal powers.

The best he could do was give himself a pep talk.

"Come on, Ethan. You can do this! You're a knight! You're brave. You are fearless!" Unfortunately, the empty words didn't have much more of an impact than those cheesy motivational posters on the walls in Mr. Corbin's history class. There was only one thing left to do . . . pray!

Before he knew it, Thursday afternoon had come and gone. The evening of the Christmas concert had arrived, and Ethan found himself standing in front of his bathroom mirror, inspecting his concert attire. His mom was packing up to head out to the car, which left him no choice.

I'm just going to tell Mrs. Hanson that I'm sick. I can't play tonight. Contemplating the validity of his excuse, Ethan surrendered in defeat. With a deep sigh he concluded, *Nope, can't do that. She saw me at school today. She'll know I'm lying. I just have to do it, I guess.*

With any hope of escape crushed by reality, Ethan resolved to potentially being the laughing stock of the entire school.

HIS PANICKED STARE towards the audience from behind the stage curtain screamed, *NOPE! I can't do this. I'm not going out there. This is my nightmare!*

Mrs. Hanson lightly touched Ethan's shoulder to get his attention, and quietly repeated her encouragement. "You're ready, Ethan. You can do this. You just need to put one foot in front of the other. You've got this."

So he did. Ethan took one step out from behind the curtain, his limp feeling more wobbly than usual. He wasn't even two steps out when he started seeing black spots in his vision.

No, not now. I will not faint! I will not faint!

The sound of applause gave Ethan a boost of focus, as if he could feed off the crowd's energy to use as his own. Approaching the microphone, he held his guitar in his left hand, keeping his pick in his pocket so he wouldn't embarrass himself by dropping it. Ironically, that strategy backfired on Ethan, but not before tripping on his guitar cable, causing his bad leg to give out, stumbling a couple feet before catching himself from going all the way down.

The audible gasp from the audience hung in the air like a dark, heavy raincloud. At any moment the entire room would burst into showers of snickering and judgment. He just knew it.

Requiring every ounce of determination Ethan possessed, he straightened and limped the rest of the way to where the mic stood ready to amplify his humiliation.

"Hello." Instant squealing filled the auditorium like a Piccolo Pete on the 4th of July, an obvious sign of failure in Ethan's eyes. He immediately pulled away from the microphone, and froze. With one deep inhale, and a silent prayer that the sound guy might be hidden somewhere in the blackness of the room, fixing the feedback, he returned to the microphone to try again.

"Hi." He paused . . . when he felt sure it would work this time, he continued, "I'm Ethan." The monitors were finally functioning properly. "I'm going to play a Christmas carol for you." As he pulled his guitar pick from his pocket, his butterfingers betrayed him, dropping the pick like he feared he would.

Reacting quickly, he bent down to pick it up, causing yet another ripple effect of embarrassment. Ethan banged his head on the microphone stand, which threatened to topple over with its swaying. Ethan steadied it with his right hand, still holding the guitar in his left, and quickly finished his descent to retrieve the pick of betrayal.

The series of unfortunate events happened in a matter of seconds, but it was plenty of time for Ethan to be mortified. The audience started murmuring and chuckling, as if Ethan was on stage performing stand-up comedy and not music. The hum of the crowd translated to instant panic for Ethan.

9

AT THIS POINT, there was nothing Ethan could do but keep going. With his guitar still in his hand, he wedged the pick between the strings on his guitar to prevent another colossal mistake. Then he finished the introduction to his song.

"This is 'Hark! The Herald Angels Sing.'"

Stepping back from the microphone to make space to put his guitar on, Ethan hesitated for a brief moment to reflect.

He closed his eyes, remembering the exact moment he first felt the strong support of his knight's metal armor around his chest. Ethan lifted his guitar over his head, securing it in place like a righteous breastplate. With his heart now protected, he could breathe in deeply, filling his lungs with a calming relief. An exhale of assurance prepared him for his next move.

Ethan opened his eyes, and stared at his feet. A single step forward propelled him into a readiness to bring a special kind of peace to his audience through his music. He could see his brown, laced-up boot leading the way, but he felt the sturdiness of a soldier's steel-toed stride as he took another step. The limp that had been his enemy for so long was now powerless to identify him.

Ethan stood before the crowd with a confidence that spoke volumes through his silent stature. He removed the pick from the security of the guitar's strings, and raised it to the instrument, like a knight raising his sword for battle.

Holding the pressure of the pick against its strings, Ethan unsheathed his weapon, piercing the night with the bold strum of his guitar. The ring of his first chord permeated every empty space in the room, capturing the guests with an awakening energy.

Instantly, a hush quieted the whispers. The movement in the crowd settled. With eyes wide, Ethan began to feel the music, remembering the joy his performance brought the king.

For the first time, his thoughts weren't interrupted with the threat of failure and embarrassment. Hundreds of people focused on him, but the music was more powerful than the fear.

It was as if Ethan played for an audience of One. He could even see the king in his royal robes standing proudly in the back of the auditorium.

There was no mistaking it. The joy his music inspired was

evident. The king's pleasure radiating from a smile so genuine gave Ethan the clarity he'd been missing.

Courage in this silent night has nothing to do with any magic from a guitar. It's the joy his music stirs in the soul of a knight that spreads to the hearts of anyone else who hears it.

Music is the magic.

The ringing from that single chord quieted to nothing, the anticipation of greatness thick in the air. Ethan closed his eyes and silently prayed. *God, I need your help.*

Immediately, he felt an extra boost of strength. Opening his eyes, he found himself looking directly into the beaming face of his mom. Her unspoken encouragement matched that of his dad who sat next to her, hand-in-hand, both grinning from ear to ear. They cheered Ethan on, as discreetly as possible, shaking their joined fist raised in excitement.

"HARK!"

The single, spoken word pierced the silence as if it had been proclaimed by the king himself. Ethan's voice continued in a tender, tenor melody.

"The herald angels sing, 'Glory to the newborn King' . . ."

His guitar's rich timbre filled in the harmonies, the music hovering on the air for a moment's ritard before saturating the entire space with the purest sound of its song.

With each verse and chorus, Ethan's rendition of the timeless

Christmas carol unified the audience into one voice. Before he knew it, everyone was singing along with him. His performance had truly taken an unexpected turn. He was actually enjoying the experience of sharing his music with others!

"Hail the heaven-born Prince of Peace!
Hail the Sun of Righteousness!
Light and life to all He brings,
risen with healing in His wings.
Mild He lays His glory by,
born that we no more may die,
born to raise us from the earth,
born to give us second birth.
Hark! The herald angels sing,
'Glory to the newborn King'"

The chorus of voices sustained past the final strum of

Ethan's guitar, holding onto that precious, reverent moment as long as possible.

Careful not to shift the setting of what had become a holy house of worship, Ethan slowly lowered the guitar down to his side.

In that moment, the audience erupted into a standing ovation of applause and cheering.

Ethan felt it, too. He knew the praise was so much more than a crowd congratulating its performer. His own internal ovation was a visceral response to his adoration of the One, True King!

THE END

A NOTE FROM THE AUTHOR

Fiction Inspired by Family

Thank you so much for joining me for Book 3 in my *Story of the Month* Newsletter Series! You are the reader I've prayed for while writing this book.

This is my middle grade fiction chapter book series inspired by my own family and articles I write on my blog. You can find all my books in this series at my online shop, or add them to your next Amazon order.

It is so enjoyable for me to find just the right cutoff for the monthly installment to provide the perfect cliffhanger. Let me know if you enjoy that part, too! I always love hearing your feedback about how these stories have impacted your life, so please reach out to me at hello@staciaraelowe.com and share!

You can read about my family's personal experience with childhood cancer in my blog, *What's the Point?* I wrote this article with the intention of bringing awareness to what family life is like with a sick child, as well as sharing hope to encourage everyone during seasons of pain and loss.

You can find more of my writings on my blog when you scan the QR code above. Be sure to join my email list so you don't miss my next *Story of the Month* to read for free! MacGyver's story will begin in the New Year! You'll also receive access to my Free Download Library, along with additional discounts and savings when you sign up!

What's the Point?

Originally published at www.StaciaRaeLowe.com
September 20, 2022

"When you reach the end of your rope, tie a knot in it and hang on."
-*Franklin D. Roosevelt*

What's the point anyway?

So much of life is just plain hard! At times it doesn't even feel worth it to hang on and let the dreams, that once mattered so much to us, take another second of our thoughts. Anything other than reality is pretty much obsolete. There has to be more than this.

And I believe there is.

When our once-upon-a-time dreams seem so much bigger than the mundane, day-to-day grind, it can feel like we're not fulfilling our calling. But I know God has a purpose for all of it, even the underwhelming stuff. So if there's purpose in all of it, what is it?

What is my purpose? Is purpose temporary? Circumstantial? Is it different than my calling? Isn't a calling supposed to be lifelong meaning? Is it the same as destiny?

Even without any answers, we can feel secure in God's faithfulness. It's okay to not have the answers. The bigger picture is that God is in control and He does have the answers. God's got it.

Especially in our pain, God will hang on.

It may not feel like it sometimes, but I truly believe there is purpose in pain. Let me tell you from experience, the painful process becomes a little more manageable if it's accompanied by the hope that my effort to endure won't be wasted.

The tears matter!

If music is a source of encouragement and renewal for you as it has always been for me, here's a song that sparks that joy and hope in me. I've been enjoying the songs of this sibling trio a lot recently.

CAIN – *Over My Head*

It could just be that God is inviting us into something bigger than ourselves. Maybe it seems impossible, but if we hang on and lean into it, we might learn to understand the value of responding to life in a way that pleases Him, despite the struggle.

> *"And so, from the day we heard, we have not ceased to pray for you, asking that you may be filled with the knowledge of his will in all spiritual wisdom and understanding, so as to walk in a manner worthy of the Lord, fully pleasing to him: bearing fruit in every good work and increasing in the knowledge of God; being strengthened with all power, according to his glorious might, for all endurance and patience with joy; giving thanks to the Father, who has qualified you to share in the inheritance of the saints in light. He has delivered us from the domain of darkness and transferred us to the kingdom of his beloved Son, in whom we have redemption, the forgiveness of sins."*
> *Colossians 1:9-14 ESV*

It has been in those moments that God has shown me his unmistakable kindness with an intentional, overwhelming awareness of his presence! My family went through a season with countless moments like this, covered in God's protection and favor.

Childhood Cancer

When your two year old stops thriving, and is near death, it's hard not to melt into a puddle of tears, paralyzed with fear and defeat. And there were definitely days of that for my husband and me. However, from the beginning, I chose to cling to God's faithfulness and sovereignty, trusting His peace that found its place in my heart.

> *"You will keep in perfect peace those whose minds are steadfast, because they trust in you. Trust in the Lord forever, for the Lord, the Lord himself, is the Rock eternal."*
> *Isaiah 26:3-4 NIV*

I trusted that my son would survive, and that God would use him to strengthen others throughout his life. I knew that the road through childhood leukemia would be scary and painful, but I didn't lose hope. Looking back with the hindsight I now have, it's clear to me how God worked this truth in the life of our son.

Ezekiel – "God will strengthen"

September is Childhood Cancer Awareness Month. So I want to invite you in, behind the scenes, to get a glimpse of what it's like to have a child with cancer, and also celebrate with us that my baby beat it!

"A picture is worth a thousand words."
So let me tell you a story . . .

[Scan the QR Code below to see the picture collage of Zeke's chemo years, included in the full blog.]

Admitted to the hospital on July 2, 2015 and diagnosed the next day, immediate blood transfusions were necessary, because he was at high risk of heart failure and system shutdown.

Zeke was 2 years & 2 months old.

His older brother Joey was 9, his younger brother MacGyver was 9 1/2 months, and the week prior to Zeke's diagnosis we'd found out I was pregnant with baby #4 – Curtis, who would join the crew 7+ months into treatment.

Steroids are rough on a little body. The belly and the face blow up like a balloon, accompanied by a ravaging appetite with insatiable cravings around the clock. Cheese…Zeke could never get enough cheese! His legs were skinny with bone damage caused by the chemo, and often couldn't support his excess weight. Plus, the two year old tantrums were still a thing. Imagine the "Terrible Twos" on   steroids…literally!

The steroids essentially would jump start his immune system. The consistent doses spiked his levels of various blood, platelet, and immunity dependent aspects of his body so that it would have a better chance of fighting the effects of not only the cancer, but the chemo as well.

Family played a significant role in the years of treatment, right from the start.

Daddy, Zeke, Auntie Faith and Uncle Tripp spent the 4th of July together watching the fireworks show from the 6th floor clinic windows on his third day of treatment. Since Zeke couldn't leave the hospital, we brought the family to him.

We developed a routine during the overnight chemo schedules. I would work remotely at the hospital with Zeke during the day while Adam worked at the office, and Grandma & Grandpa watched the two brothers. Then we would all meet for dinner in Zeke's room, followed by the shift change. Dad would spend the night with Zeke, and Mom would take the brothers home.

This is when Dad's journaling began, eventually turning into ***Ezekiel's Path: Our Family's Walk Through Childhood Leukemia***. Before we knew it (my pregnancy was a blur), Baby Brother's first visit to the pediatric oncology clinic to stay with Mommy and Big Brother was when he was 3 days old, and he quickly became a favorite chemo companion.

Clinic days and Peds floor stays were exhausting and incredibly boring. After watching "Frozen" or "Monster's Inc." for the third consecutive viewing in a twelve hour period

Every. Single. Day.

. . . as the yellow miracle poison slowly dripped, everyone in attendance would be feeling a little stir crazy! But there were only so many times you could take a lap in the wagon around the pediatric department before the "outing" lost its appeal. Any ideals of limited screen time went completely out the window from the time of our first extended stay.

However, as draining and discouraging as the 3 1/2 years of treatment could be, our doctors, nurses and social workers never failed to bring smiles enough to share!

A HUGE thank you to our Kaiser family!

You all played such a meaningful and invaluable part in Zeke's story. We love you!

And if you hadn't already noticed, Tobey (the giraffe) might have been Zeke's biggest, most constant source of comfort and love.

Here are some of Adam's thoughts during those difficult treatment days, from one of his articles.

". . . It had been a very difficult night at the hospital for Zeke. He'd recently been added to the "high risk for relapse" list and so his treatment had to be switched around and intensified, which made for longer stays at the hospital and more extreme treatment, which just made everything all around more difficult, uncomfortable, and more painful in general.

This particular day was after multiple nights in the hospital, lying awake as Zeke slept. During that whole first year, whenever Zeke had to stay overnight (which felt more often than not), I'd often just lie awake writing in my journal, which eventually led to the book I published, Ezekiel's Path. So, after multiple sleepless nights of nurses coming in every hour to check vitals and the sound of medical equipment beeping and whirring, Stacia arrived at the hospital so I could go to work . . . and that is when I heard that song for the first time.

I remember feeling like walking death, super exhausted, horribly emotionally bankrupt, and just feeling about as hopeless as possible . . . when those opening lyrics [of this song] hit me . . .

MercyMe – *Even If*

Those years were incredibly difficult. But it's evident how God used this season to bring such intentional purpose and meaning into our lives."

If you want to watch the video we shared at Zeke's party to celebrate the end of his chemo treatment, check it out here:

Our boys have recently started a YouTube channel @lowebudgetkids. They have been having so much fun creating videos for you to enjoy! If you're encouraged by their music or have a good laugh at their humor and shenanigans, would you please consider subscribing? They are working toward their goal of gaining 2,000 subscribers!

ABOUT THE AUTHOR

After working many years in public and private accounting, Stacia is now self-employed as an accounting consultant for several small businesses, including homeschool co-ops and a STEM learning center. This is where she also teaches knitting plus budgeting to homeschool students throughout the school year.

Knot Your Average Knitting is very possibly the only knitting class where students learn how to knit, while also learning how to responsibly afford their current and future hobbies using a family budget!

Her love for writing began during her years as a single mom with pen pal letters to her brother's friend. That friend is now her husband, and together they write books to share the Hope of Christ, because He is the One who inspires their words.

Stacia is passionate about writing stories of God's redemption in her books. It's her desire to share her work and entrepreneurial perspective in an effort to cultivate connection, peace of mind for moms, and a Hope for the future!

MORE BOOKS

by

Stacia Rae Lowe
& Adam Alva Lowe

FICTION

Fiction Inspired by Family Collection
In Between Tall and Small: Story of the Month Book 2
Again & Again: Story of the Month Book 1
The Toymaker's Dream

NONFICTION

Stop Staying Stuck:
Taking That First Step Into Financial Peace of Mind

Hidden Hope:
Finding Hope Through Trials and Loss

Heated to Completion:
A Devotional for Encouraging Wisdom and Growth

Ezekiel's Path:
Our Family's Walk Through Childhood Leukemia

www.ingramcontent.com/pod-product-compliance
Lightning Source LLC
Chambersburg PA
CBHW071541100726
47908CB00004B/1458